Croc
by the
Rock

For Charlotte and Samuel

First published 2005
Evans Brothers Limited
2A Portman Mansions
Chiltern St
London W1U 6NR

Text copyright © Hilary Robinson 2005
© in the illustrations Mike Gordon 2005
Additional illustration work by Carl Gordon

British Library Cataloguing in Publication Data

Robinson, Hilary
        Croc by the rock. – (Zig zag)
        1. Children's stories – Pictorial works
        I. Title
        823.9'14 [J]

ISBN 0237529513
13-digit ISBN (from 1 January 2007) 9780237529512

Printed in China by WKT Company Ltd

Series Editor: Nick Turpin
Design: Robert Walster
Production: Jenny Mulvanny
Series Consultant: Gill Matthews

ZIG ZAG

Croc by the Rock

by Hilary Robinson

illustrated by Mike Gordon

When Jake took his net...

...to fish by the rock

6

he saw what he thought...

8

...was the eye of a croc!

10

"A croc by the rock!"
Jake called to the man...

11

...who let his dog out

from the back of a van.

The dog stretched his paws

then raced round the rock...

...then jumped in the lake

to hunt for the croc!

He dipped and he dived

as the kids rushed to take...

...some photographs of

the croc in the lake.

Then everyone cheered

as the dog showed to all...

...that the crocodile's eye

was only a ball!

But later that day

Jake fished on the rock...

...and found in his net...

...a tooth from a croc!

Why not try reading another ZigZag book?

Dinosaur Planet   ISBN: 0 237 52667 0
by David Orme and Fabiano Fiorin

Tall Tilly   ISBN: 0 237 52668 9
by Jillian Powell and Tim Archbold

Batty Betty's Spells   ISBN: 0 237 52669 7
by Hilary Robinson and Belinda Worsley

The Thirsty Moose   ISBN: 0 237 52666 2
by David Orme and Mike Gordon

The Clumsy Cow   ISBN: 0 237 52656 5
by Julia Moffatt and Lisa Williams

Open Wide!   ISBN: 0 237 52657 3
by Julia Moffatt and Anni Axworthy

Too Small   ISBN 0 237 52777 4
by Kay Woodward and Deborah van de Leijgraaf

I Wish I Was An Alien   ISBN 0 237 52776 6
by Vivian French and Lisa Williams

The Disappearing Cheese   ISBN 0 237 52775 8
by Paul Harrison and Ruth Rivers

Terry the Flying Turtle   ISBN 0 237 52774 X
by Anna Wilson and Mike Gordon

Pet To School Day   ISBN 0 237 52773 1
by Hilary Robinson and Tim Archbold

The Cat in the Coat   ISBN 0 237 52772 3
by Vivian French and Alison Bartlett

Pig in Love   ISBN 0 237 52950 5
by Vivian French and Tim Archbold

The Donkey That Was Too Fast   ISBN 0 237 52949 1
by David Orme and Ruth Rivers

The Yellow Balloon   ISBN 0 237 52948 3
by Helen Bird and Simona Dimitri

Hamish Finds Himself   ISBN 0 237 52947 5
by Jillian Powell and Belinda Worsley

Flying South   ISBN 0 237 52946 7
by Alan Durant and Kath Lucas

Croc by the Rock   ISBN 0 237 52945 9
by Hilary Robinson and Mike Gordon

32